THE WoLF AND THE BABY DRAGoN

Avril McDonald

Illustrated

Crown House Publishing Limited
www.crownhouse.co.uk

First published by

Crown House Publishing Ltd
Crown Buildings, Bancyfelin, Carmarthen, Wales, SA33 5ND, UK
www.crownhouse.co.uk

and

Crown House Publishing Company LLC
PO Box 2223, Williston, VT 05495
www.crownhousepublishing.com

Illustrations by Tatiana Minina

First published 2016. Reprinted 2017.

British Library Cataloguing-in-Publication Data
A catalogue entry for this book is available from the British Library.

Print ISBN: 978-178583021-1
Mobi ISBN: 978-178583098-3
ePub ISBN: 978-178583099-0
ePDF ISBN: 978-178583100-3

LCCN 2015953333

Printed and bound in the UK by
Gomer Press, Llandysul, Ceredigion

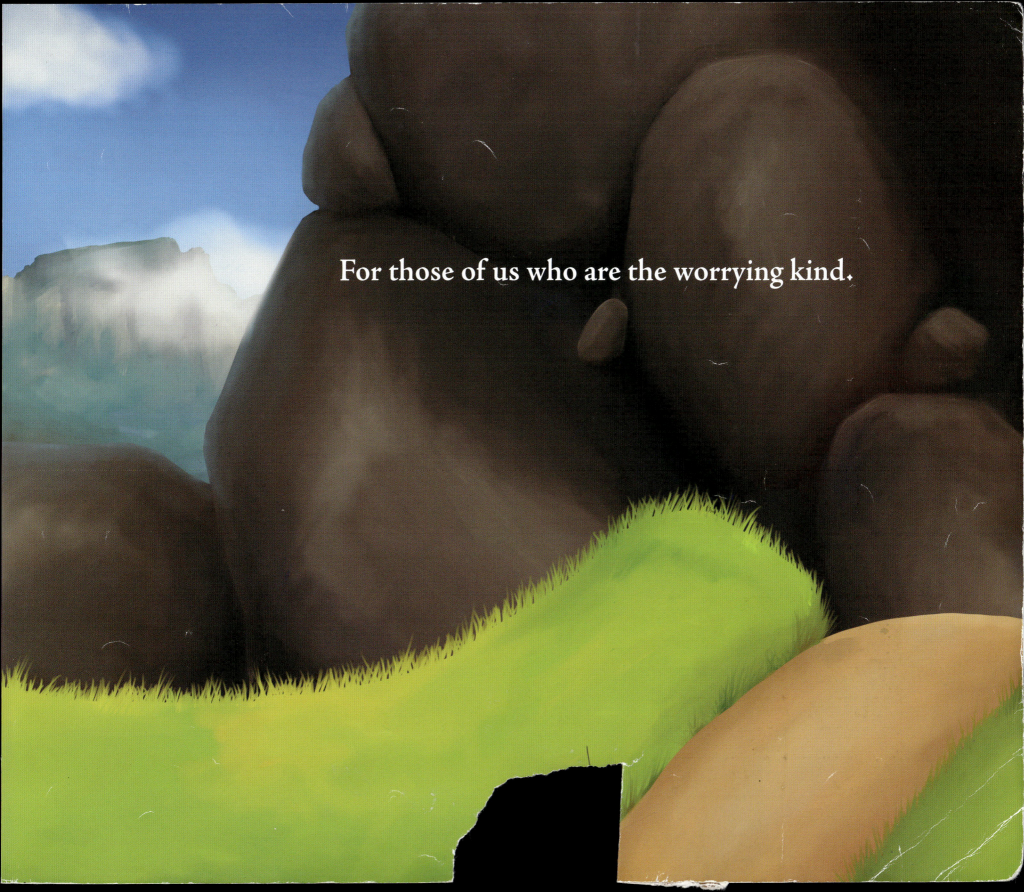

For those of us who are the worrying kind.

Thanks to Åsa Pettersson for her inspiration and contribution to Feel Brave's work and to the poet Robert Saxton for his editorial directive.

Deep in the forest
at the tree house one day
Montgomery had something
important to say.

He had heard of a cave,
far away to the west,
Where a new baby dragon
had hatched in a nest.

"We should go there," he said,
"we could have such great fun."
"Oh we *must*," said Catreen,
"get your things. Quick, let's run!"

So they filled up their bags
     with some nice things to eat:
Some water to drink
     and some fudge for a treat.

Then marched off in a hurry
with dragons in mind,
But forgetting poor Wolfgang ...
who got left behind.

His bag was so heavy
it made him too slow.
Missing out on the dragon
would bother him so.

He yelled, "Wait for me!"
No one heard him at all:
They were too far ahead
and his voice was too small.

Then he tripped on a rock
   and fell down with a thump.
On the top of his head
   grew a mighty great lump.

He had worries he couldn't
   stop thinking about,
That he'd packed in his bag
   and wouldn't let out.

He had always found worries
   too hard to let go
And he kept them a secret –
   his friends didn't know.

He had never had worries
so heavy before,
Which is why he just couldn't
go on any more.

So he lay on the ground
under one big dark cloud.
Then something quite small
called his name out quite loud.

"Wolfgang," said Spider,
    from high in the tree,
"I know of your secret,
    it's safe here with me.

We all have our worries,
    some big and some small,
But too many worries
    are no good at all!

I can see you're unhappy,
    it's easy to tell.
Take a rest for a while
    with this magical spell ..."

"Stars in the night gather near
Fairies fly and meet us here.
As we close our eyes and count to ten,
Breathe in and out and in again.

Wiggle your toes ... now make a smile.
Be very still and think a while ...

Who do you love and who loves you?
What's your favourite thing to do?
Where's the best place you've ever been?
What's the most magical thing you've seen?
Stir all these things around in your cup
And like a hot chocolate, drink them all up!"

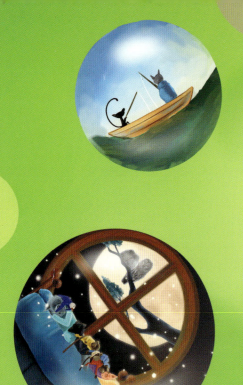

It was lovely to think about
things that were good.
He'd have done it all day
if only he could.

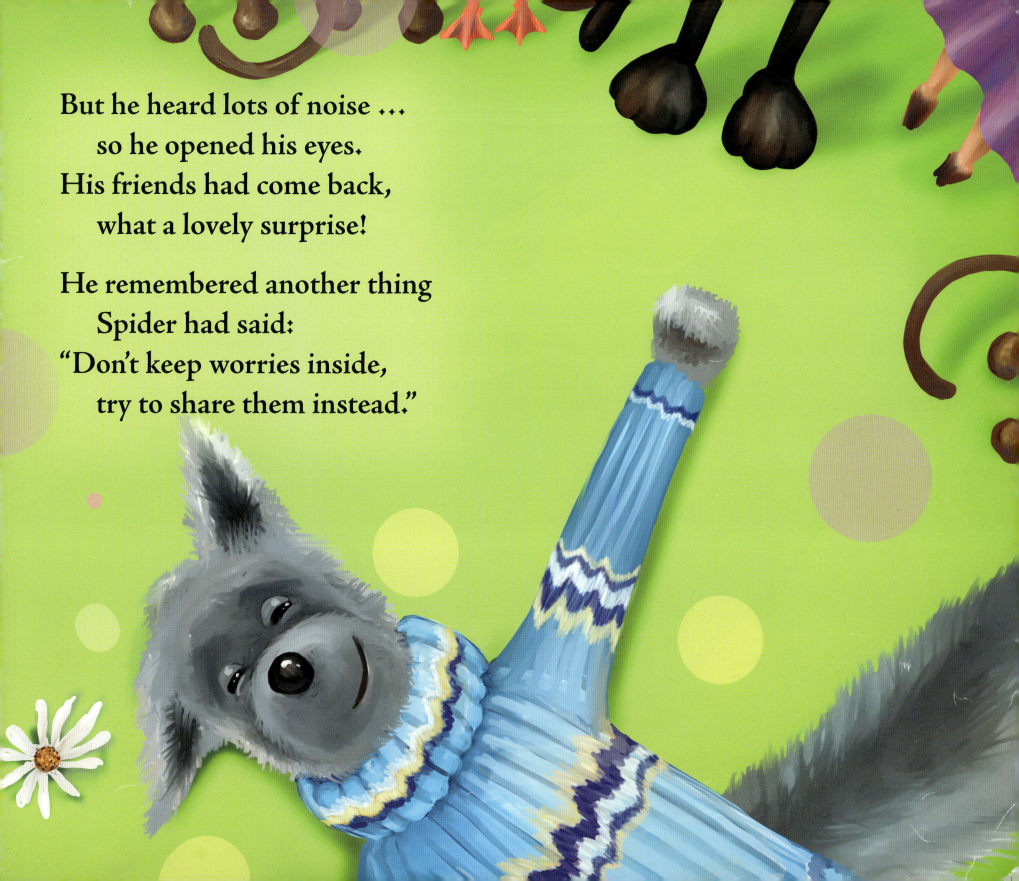

But he heard lots of noise …
    so he opened his eyes.
His friends had come back,
    what a lovely surprise!

He remembered another thing
    Spider had said:
"Don't keep worries inside,
    try to share them instead."

"Hey Wolfgang," they cried.
      "Funny thing! There you are!
We've found where the cave is.
      Up there! It's not far."

"Oh I do want to come
      but my bag makes me slow.
It's full of my worries,
      I can't let them go."

"Well we'll help you carry them,"
said Daisy Pig.
"We could all take one each
so your bag's not so big.

You might have some worries
that we've all had too.
If you share them with us
we might know what to do."

So they emptied his worries
out onto the ground …
They were all quite surprised
at how many they found.

But they managed to sort them,
and each friend took one.
Now the bag wasn't heavy
and Wolfgang could run.

They ran like the wind
up the rocks to the cave.

Wolfgang felt loved ...
and a little more brave.

When they got to the top,
    their hearts skipped a beat –
There it was in the cave,
    looking snuggly and sweet.

But just as they spotted
two cute fluffy paws …
A great beast flew above them
with frightful sharp claws!

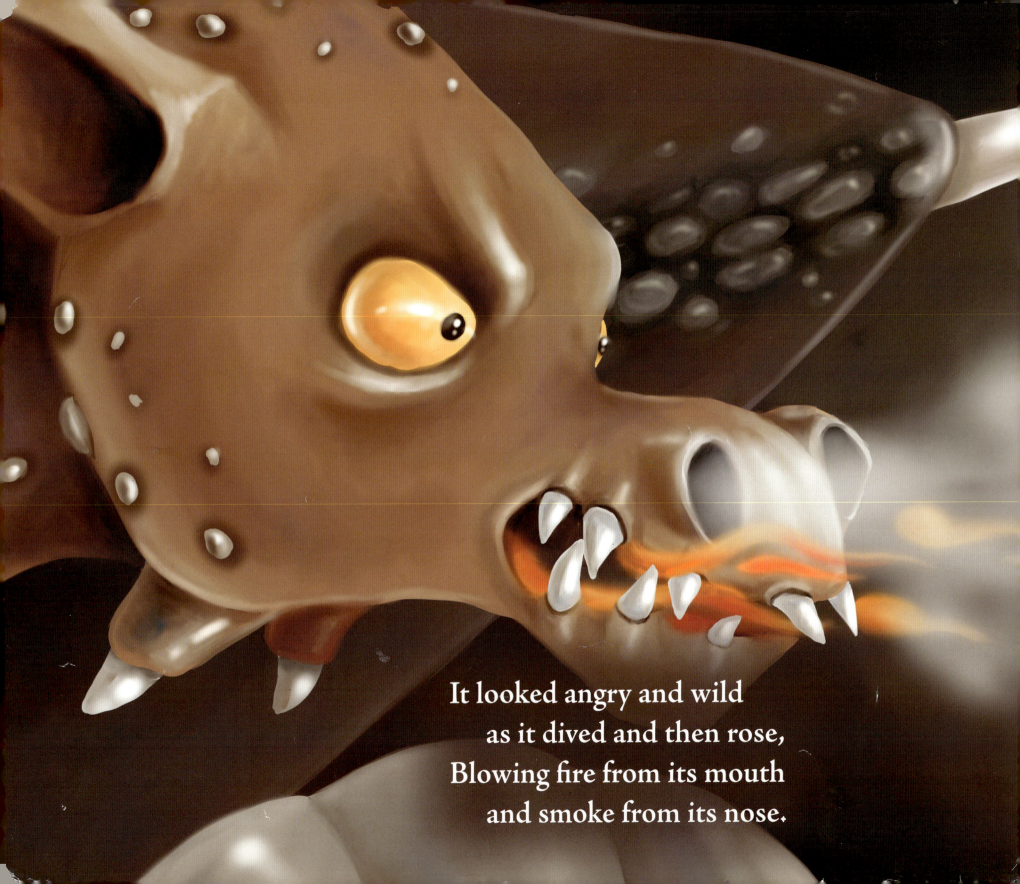

It looked angry and wild
as it dived and then rose,
Blowing fire from its mouth
and smoke from its nose.

There was certainly no chance
of getting away ...
It was likely that they'd all
be eaten that day!

But the dragon did not
 want to have them for tea:
It just wanted to take
 all their worries, you see.

For a new baby dragon
 loves nothing more
Than to have some cute cuddly
 friends to adore.

Most worries seem ugly
but they didn't mind:
These dragons were just
not the worrying kind.

They all laughed loudly
and jumped with delight!

(Which happens sometimes
when you've had a big fright.)

Then back at the tree house
they all felt so glad.
To be eaten by dragons …
that would have been bad!

They decided to try
      Wolfgang's new magic spell,
So the stars and the fairies
      all joined them as well.

And their little hearts glowed
as their minds took a rest,
While the evening sun set,
far away to the west.